Adam Wallace & Chris Kennett

DAD JOKES ARE THE BEST

WORST!

Scholastic Canada Ltd.
Toronto New York London Auckland Sydney
Mexico City New Delhi Hong Kong Buenos Aires

For Dad, in memory of the kid who only had ears!
Thank you for your jokes and your friendship. — AW

To my dad, Colin.
Thanks for giving me your silly sense of humour! x — CK

Scholastic Australia
An imprint of Scholastic Australia Pty Limited
PO Box 579 Gosford NSW 2250
ABN 11 000 614 577

Scholastic Canada Ltd.
604 King Street West, Toronto, Ontario M5V 1E1, Canada

Scholastic Inc.
557 Broadway, New York, NY 10012, USA

Scholastic Australia Pty Limited
PO Box 579, Gosford, NSW 2250, Australia

Scholastic New Zealand Limited
Private Bag 94407, Botany, Manukau 2163, New Zealand

Scholastic Children's Books
Euston House, 24 Eversholt Street, London NW1 1DB, UK

www.scholastic.ca

Library and Archives Canada Cataloguing in Publication

Title: Dad jokes are the worst! / Adam Wallace & Chris Kennett.
Names: Wallace, Adam, author. | Kennett, Chris, illustrator.
Identifiers: Canadiana 20210257121 | ISBN 9781443194327 (softcover)
Classification: LCC PZ7.1.W35 Dad 2022 | DDC j813/.6—dc23

First published by Scholastic Australia in 2021.
This edition published by Scholastic Canada Ltd. In 2022.
Text copyright © 2021 by Adam Wallace.
Illustrations copyright © 2021 by Chris Kennett.
All rights reserved.

6 5 4 3 2 1   Printed in China CP171   22 23 24 25 26

It's **Father's Day,** and my dad rocks.
He really is **the best!**

Except for his **terrible** dad jokes . . .
I wish he'd give them a rest.

The other day, as we left the house —
how's this for **really** bad —
Mom said she'd call him **later.** He said,

I give Dad flowers
as a gift; he does a
happy dance.

Then waters them
and says to me,

LOOK! I wet
my **plants!**

I groan and **shake** my head.
Dad gives a **panicked shout.**

"Don't shake
your head!"
he cries.

What if
your **brains**
fall out?

As we get ready for the beach,
Dad tells us about his dream,

where he went to a **haunted beach** and ate
sand-witches and **ice-screeeeeeeam!**

"Can you make **me** a sandwich?" I ask...
then quickly regret what I said.

"You're a sandwich!" Dad cries,
holding **bread** against my head!

Finally, we're on our way,
and Dad **sings** as he drives along.

He thinks it's **super** funny
to sing every single word **wrong!**

Dad says, starting to drive faster.

"Where?" I say. "Too late!" he cries.

"We've already gone **pasta!**"

Mom asks Dad the time.
"Time for a new **watch,"** he says with glee.

And as soon as we get to the beach he shouts,

HEY!
Long time,
no **sea!**

He buys a drink, and the server asks,
"Want that drink **in a bag?**"

"No, thanks," Dad says. "Leave it **in the bottle.**"
My shoulders start to sag.

We dig in the sand, then I say, "I'm hot!"
"Hi, Hot," is Dad's reply.

Dad's jokes make me want to cry.

"Anyway," he adds, "it's good to be hot.
Hot's **faster** than cold, for sure.
I know this 'cause you can **catch** a cold."

"Please, Dad," I beg.

"NO MORE!"

Mom says I need a haircut when my bangs hang down too far.

"Guess how **sheep** get haircuts?" Dad asks.
"They visit the BaaaaaBaaaaaa!"

It's nearly time to head on home,
so we search rock pools for fish.
Dad's sure crabs won't share their pools,
because they are **shellfish!**

On the way back to the car,
Dad turns to us with a sigh.

"The ocean will **really** miss us.
Look at it **wave** goodbye."

And even as we're driving home,
Dad is still **chatting** away.
"Hey, kids! Would you come to the beach
if it wasn't a **SUN**day?"

That night, Dad tucks me into bed
and says **he'll love me forever.**
Every day's his **favourite**
when we are all **together.**

I know that all of Dad's jokes are
super, super bad . . .
But that's one reason **I love** him,
because it's part of what makes him

my dad!